FSC
www.fsc.org
MIXTO
Papel procedente de
fuentes responsables
Paper from
responsible sources
FSC® C105338

<u>**Copyright and traduction**</u>

© Isidro Canal Valero, 2025
Editorial: BoD · Books on Demand,
Calle de Manzanares, 4, 28005 Madrid,
bod@bod.com.es
Impresión: Libri Plureos GmbH,
Friedensallee 273, 22763 Hamburg
(Alemania)
ISBN: 978-84-1373-984-7

About the writer:

My name is Isidro Canal, an ordinary man, perhaps too much so, a 40-year-old father of two small children, Quim and Nil.

Life gave me the gift of osteoarthritis of the hip, at the early age of 36.

Operated on my spine and with a bilateral hip prosthesis pending insertion under my tissues. What the world saw as a misfortune, for me became the best thing I have found along the way, even if it began to wobble dangerously and forced me to turn my life around, to understand pain, to know that even though it is difficult, it is possible to live with its company.

To enjoy what is not important, to play down the importance of things that are not enjoyable.

At last... to learn to live with that horrendous burden, a backpack full of pain.

NOBODY WILL WALK FOR YOU

CHAPTER: N
Nobody will walk for you

This story would begin at a random time, in a random place. Just that very day, at that exact bloody hour...

The streets were no longer full of passers-by, the sound of car engines were no longer heard, the light from the street lamps had conquered the pavements and the sun had long since gone into free fall, as if dozing off amongst the treeson the horizon.

A few minutes, maybe more, had passed since sunset on that night of 7 July, when I was preparing to put my eldest s11on, four-year-old Quim, to sleep.

Everything seemed to be going absolutely normally, in a common and typical way, exhausted from a long day's work and my son, as always, fighting against his own eyelids, which were struggling to close, whilst he was fighting to keep them open.

After a while, and with my patience stretched to its limit, sleep finally overcame him. It had been a day that seemed endless, but what was to follow next would unknowingly take hold of me, making it even longer.

In the twilight of that seventh of July, like Allan Poe's raven, one or several thoughts, with their recurring and constant fluttering, never ceasing in their eagerness to fly over my head, various reflections, one after the other, voracious clouds, seemed to form over me.

After a lifetime dedicated to sport, I was diagnosed with osteoarthritis of the hip at the age of 37.

My son, at that time, lay anaesthetised by the darkness, by the rhythmic sound of crickets, in a deep and pleasant sleep.

Meanwhile, with every minute, insomnia took over me more and more, it embraced me, it was like a demanding mistress who would not leave me for a moment.

The raven returned and with it, a thousand doubts, a thousand thoughts.

The present? Dark.

The future? Uncertain.

The past? Forgotten.

That bird, jet black, camouflaged in the night, like vermin, stalking from the darkness, seemed to repeat over and over again, in its guttural voice, thou shalt not walk, thou shalt not walk.

It was easy to fall into such a thought,

My life had changed completely, it would change completely, just that night.

I had osteoarthritis, anxiety and insomnia that morning. Nothing I had would define who I am, nothing would hold me back, nothing would make me stronger.

Life put stones in the way, so as not to make it so boring or so I thought.

I tried to convince myself that it would always be like that, I tried to protect myself from something that didn't exist at that moment, but that was slowly approaching, I was entering a battlefield unknown to me and mine.

Soon, I would discover that in all wars, there are no winners, only defeated and death.

Soon and without being able to avoid it, I would enter

into a vast world I had never encountered before.

I would set my first foot on the
he ground and before my eyes would,
very dry wasteland behind the mist, a
boundless universe dark and bleak,
called pain.

CHAPTER I
The ground is lava

Slowly the hours passed and the light of a new day, appeared, lazily overcoming the darkness, a new sun arose over the horizon, after a night that had seemed endless.
The street lights ceased, the crowd with its murmurs began to throng the streets, the stars became more and more invisible by the contrast of the morning glow and with it, like a luminous lighthouse or beacon, my eyes slowly flickered to life.
I could hardly remember any thoughts of that night, or rather the hours before, I had seen them and greeted them with my eyes, each and every

one of them, and impassively they never greeted me back.
An unhealthy amnesia took hold of me and no matter how hard I tried, something or someone had reset my head.
The sun rose again, like every day, I thought it was going to be just another awakening like the usual ones.
Everything seemed to indicate that the birth of a new morning would bring nothing new with respect to the previous one, except sleep, the son of the insomnia I had suffered that morning.
The usual daily routines like so many others, the smell of coffee, waking up my children, getting them dressed, a chocolate biscuit for breakfast and the usual rush.
But nothing could be further from the truth,
The night with its dark and long claw,

gave me without knowing it, a powerful crack in my left hip, almost four centimetres long, which I didn't even notice when I was in my 'after meridian' lethargy.

Suddenly, as I placed my left foot on the ground, a resounding crunch, which sounded more like the embarrassed sobbing of the last soldier standing, sounded thunderous, dry and gritty at the same time.

The floor turned into lava, an undescribable pain, came out of nowhere and wanted to stay. A burning that quickly ran centimetre by centimetre through every stretch of my skin, as if it were the last, from my toes to my abdomen.

Namaste, son of a bitch, the arthrosis woke up from its long lethargy, sweeping through my life and my state of health.

A state that until that precise moment
I believed to be unshakable, all my life
I had a kind of Hercules syndrome.
At that precise moment, that being
that I used to recognise in front of the
mirror, vanished, that was no longer
me, it was as if all the particles of my
body had been destroyed at the speed
of light, turning me into a mass of
flesh impossible to recognise, an icy
sweat ran down my forehead due to
the effort of that first step, a mixture
of salt and water, poisoned, that
combined with the burning in my head
and the cold of my forehead at the
same time, as fever arose.
That first step was like crossing the
damned Rubicon, the ground burned,
My feet fell apart, while my hips
seemed trapped and choked tightly by
wire and broken glass that pierced and
cut me cell by cell.
A cold but fiery war, just beginning, in

which for the moment there was too little blood and too much misery.

I looked around me, I was by the bed, but the pain, the tears and the gloom did not allow me to look for a saviour, I was alone in that room, accompanied by the horrible silence that no one ever wants to hear.

My children were asleep and they didn't deserve to see me like that, they didn't deserve to wake up that way, I was no longer their father or their hero, I couldn't appear in front of them as a defeated being in that battle that had just begun and that its first minute was already devastating.

My body was shaking, my heart was racing, everything was going wrong, never in my life had I shouted so much, making so little noise, a mute sound that did not come from my dry mouth, nor from my cracked lips, but in my head, it sounded thunderous.

A shrill, metallic, rusty and dull sound at the same time, an absurd and ashamed silence that took hold of me and that did not let me think clearly, I had only taken one step and lived one minute of that war, but the ground burned, burned aggressively and tore the flesh from my feet.

There was nothing heroic in that deed, only death and desolation, in that vast wasteland.

A dirty and visceral war, a battlefield with the smell of entrails, but without a single drop of blood, for the moment.

One step, on the ground that no one wants to step on.

I had only taken one step, but the ground... turned to fiery lava.

Every step I tried to take was an act of futility, I couldn't move, only burn on the spot, burning and unable to do anything about it.

CHAPTER II
Crimson Red.

That was a great step for man, but invisible to the rest of mankind. I had never felt so alone, so mute, even with my house full of living beings.

The suffering I was enduring at that moment, would not appear on any television channel, newspaper or radio, it was an odyssey like that of Ulysses, with the difference that mine would never be remembered, or maybe it would, with your help my dear reader.

As if it were a divine sign, interpreted by a Greek soldier. An intense orange light began to tinge the room, conquering it, making it its own and illuminating the most absolute emptiness.

The first rays of the sun, that signal emitted by the mighty god Apollo, unstoppable, were pouring through the holes in the shutters.

It was like a lighthouse on the high seas, which you must use as a guide to avoid hitting land.

I took that sign, emitted by our star king as what it was, a sign that urged me to go ahead, to be brave and do what ever possible at that precise moment. More fear provoked me, but the time had come to take a second step, the sun ordered it, life demanded it of me.

I took it, with fear and leaving to chance what would follow next in that damned room.

My hip couldn't take it and because of that mechanical failure I fell to the floor, the taste of rust appeared, the suffering was so fierce that my fangs penetrated without any difficulty into the flesh of my lips, making them bleed, in an exacerbated way. My mouth, pale and thirsty from the early hour, from the pain, from the din of battle, was stained with blood, stained a deep crimson red.

Now everything was a real battlefield, in an instant all the ingredients were mixed and the pain was joined by blood and with it, the taste of the ground.

I fell against the tiles of the room, on myself, with a hip unable to support my weight, nor the weight of gravity itself, my body slammed against the floor with an inordinate and unjust fury.

Precisely that fury, that blow, those thousand stones, which seemed to fall, at the same time, on the burning cement, that wire choking and

breaking every piece of pelvis, those
thousand pieces of broken and dirty
glass cutting cleanly every centimetre
of my hip, dismembering it, piece by
piece, made a powerful signal for help
echo from the deepest part of my
entrails.
The silence of the morning was
interrupted by a scream that seemed
to stop time, to freeze the weather,
even in the middle of summer.
That indomitable, cold and dry scream
put my wife, Maria, on alert, her name
was spelt without an accent,
since that was how she was baptised
and registered in the Civil Registry.
Thus, Maria 'without a tilde' appeared
quickly in the bedroom where my
cracked body lay.
Stupefied, she could not gestate any
words, nor could she help me much,
she only found a broken body, on a
floor that was too barren.

Ulysses had landed in Ithaca but there was nothing glorious in that two-step crossing, full of hardship and destitution.

A desolate voyage, whose main characters were very different from those we usually imagine. Right here and now there were no troops, weapons, ships and honor.

A journey that ended in the worst of ways, almost lifeless, with the clothes worn out by the battle.

A single minute was enough to be unable to fill it with sixty seconds of tireless struggle. An unconscienscious and totally unbiased agony, it took just under three seconds to defeat his opponent.

My journey ended on the floor of a narrow alley, between the bed and the wall, dark, surrounded by blood, rust, metallic air, stinging eyes, drowning in my own tears.

There was no greatness in that journey that I ended, begging to myself, in that improvised battlefield, where the first rays of the sun of that damned morning, pierced through the holes of the shutter, projecting disturbingly mysterious reddish flashes. Beams of light that seemed to float in the air, illuminating particles of dust that danced silently over my body.

CHAPTER III
The Road to Italy

My children were still asleep, whilt my wife listened to the whimpers of a wounded and abandoned soldier in the middle of a mission, the kind where there are no medals, decorations or flags.

The destination of my mission was not to land heroically on a beach under mortar fire, nor to fight in a Roman coliseum for glory, but only to reach the car, the lifeboat, that would take me to seek medical assistance and, at last, salvation.

Every step towards the door became hell, a desolate Hades, of pain, of tears, of blood already parched.

A sharp, acidic pain seemed to course through every vein in my body.
Arteries at maximum capacity, trying to hold the blood of a racing heart, pumping harder and harder and more and more fatigued.
The beats were like bombs falling, hitting my ribs, I could feel the skin dancing on them, ribs that kept trying their best to contain their blood core inside my chest.
I could taste the taste of entrails on my tongue. My own, trying as hard as I could, to get out from between my teeth, I covered my mouth as best I could with my hand to keep them inside me, as I approached the exit door, crawling towards my car, towards my lifeboat.
I opened the door and the powerful sun dazzled me for a few moments while, with my other hand, I tried to hold on to the wall, railing or any

moderately stable object that was capable of avoiding a new fall into hell.

Fifteen metres, which seemed like miles, separated me from my vehicle; I have to admit that this was my first act of bravery.

I should have called an ambulance, but it was too late, I wasn't going to throw away all the work I had done so far.

My body was fighting, I was fighting and my brain started to conceive beta endorphins to try and fight the pain from head-to-toe. But it was an affront that I knew I would not win, a one-way mission, but not a return, suffering always has more and better ammunition, more troops and the worst thing, it has no compassion, it doesn't care about dying if it can kill, for pleasure, for satisfaction...; it doesn't matter.

I shuffled to the car, each step a lost battle against the pain that pierced me like a dagger. My hip, fragile and broken by arthrosis, gave way under the weight of my body, betraying me with every movement. A cold sweat ran down my forehead, mingling with the tears that fell uncontrollably, silently, as witnesses to my surrender. The pain was unbearable, but I kept moving as best I could. Clinging to the car door as if it were my only salvation. Each step cost me more than the last, as if my hip, cowardly and defeated, refused to fight on, exhausted by the suffering.

As I settled into the driver's seat, acid again,

gnawing at me again.

I couldn't understand how such a simple act as sitting in front of the steering wheel could make me feel as if a thousand rats were nibbling at the

bone of an open wound, unwilling to
cease their activity, feeding on my
bloody flesh.
I started the engine of my car,
I went all the way between first and
second gear.
Each step on the clutch pedal was like
rubbing against a burning ember, each
step on the pedal was as if I had
become a yolk.
as if I had become an anvil and an
inordinately excited blacksmith was
beating me over and over again.
That bastard wanted to mould me with
his craftsman's hammer, taking
advantage of me and my molten,
nibbling hips at hundreds of degrees.
After countless minutes of constant
hammering and insufferable pain I
arrived at the emergency room.
I don't remember how I managed to
get there, park, or make my way to
the door, without my soul leaving me,

never mind.
I got my second medal, one of those medals that your loved ones will never see, but that I will try to remember forever.

Fuck yeah! I made it to the hospital.

 I thought with painful joy.
Once I put on the 'all inclusive' bracelet with my medical history printed on it, I knew I would have no limit of painkillers, therapeutic drugs, no needles… I was salivating with pleasure, I am no drug addict and I have never taken drugs but I craved it, I needed it, I wanted the moment to come when they would inject something into my skin to give me a trip that would relieve the pain, I wanted more than anything in the world, a good shot that would be really inhibiting.

I arrived with a fever, a high fever, and was presented with a welcome Paracetamol;

Both the health professional and I knew that it would have no effect, that it would be like trying to stop a bullet train with a wall of aluminium foil and that behind him, he would be kneeling on the track on which the train was travelling and would not think of slowing down.
Sitting, in any way that seemed to me more or less compatible with life, in one of those 'stretcher chairs' that they put in the corridors of emergency rooms nowadays, I waited anxiously for someone to arrive, with my dose, my gender, I had been on a fucking Paracetamol for thirty minutes and it didn't do any good.
Suddenly I heard...

Buongiorno! said a nurse.

I don't remember her name, only that she was a trainee and that she was from Bergamo.

I do remember that she had her partner Luca, who came to live with her and that they were drawing on the savings they had accumulated in Italy, so that they could come to finish their internship and look for a job near Barcelona.

A fucking exchange student, who seemed to know very little about what she was doing, proceeded to give me an IV.

Nerves and pain made me think like that and I regret it, we have all gone through similar processes to that student and we have all failed in order to learn.

Like a good apprentice, she stuck the sharp needle into one of my veins and like a good apprentice, she stuck the

IV in without closing the valve, which administers the longed-for drug.

A stream of dark, rusty blood stained the whole place, it had turned into a bloody horror movie, while 'Bergamo', the name I would give to the nurse, tried to control a situation that appeared unexpectedly and to which she was not used to, a situation in which you can suddenly find yourself and that should be contemplated in the studies.

Blood is slippery and Bergamo discovered it that day, with her feet on the thick liquid, she skidded and on her knees on the floor, stained by the insatiable plasma that came out of the track, she tried to get up, I feel sorry for her, but that bloody and violent rape, filled me with a pleasurable revenge, that made me forget the pain, although not for more than an instant.

Already recomposed and bathed in my
fluid, she arranged her hair, looked me
in the eyes and after having shared
that instant, that almost sexual act,
Bergamo left without further ado,
without apology, it was as if my skin
had been transmuted into that of Jack
the Ripper and she fled from me, in a
mixture of fear and shame, but not
before injecting me with the perfect
formula.
A chemical mixture of opiates and
anti-inflammatories.
She and I finished at the same time,
and after that obscene barbecue.
She left without a word or a glance,
she abandoned me after that intense
relationship.

I never saw Bergamo again.

CHAPTER IV
Trick or treat

The drive back was a blur, a void in my mind. I don't remember putting my hands on the steering wheel or feeling the feel of the seat under my body. Just the hum of the engine in the background, monotonous and distant, as if it belonged to another world. The streets passed around me, but I couldn't see them, enveloped in a thick haze of scattered thoughts. The landscape faded into fragments, choppy, as the lights flickered meaninglessly. Without knowing how, I found myself in front of my house, with the keys still in the ignition, but with no memory of the road travelled, as if the car had been guided by an alien force, while I remained absent, trapped in an amnesiac limbo.

I opened the car door with clumsy, almost automatic movements, as if my body was operating on instinct and my mind was still trapped in a dense fog. The steps to my house were slow and hesitant, each one heavier than the last. The world around me seemed distant, blurred, as if it wasn't real. I crossed the threshold of the door without remembering doing so, my hands brushing the walls to guide me, searching for something solid to hold me up. Finally, I reached my room, dropped onto the bed, the mattress taking me in a silent embrace. My body sank into the sheets, unable to move any further, as if I had finally found the refuge I had been searching for. I lay there, no clear thoughts, just the overwhelming weight of fatigue and dull ache in the background, surrendered to the darkness and fell asleep.

The first thing I remember when I opened my eyes, was the white colour of the ceiling of the double bedroom where I lay.

A deep white that seemed to have no end. I had never thought about it before, but it reminded me of space, but with inverted colours, a totally white and infinite cosmos.

I guess the magic potion they injected me with at the hospital had the expected effect. Although I would have preferred not to return home accompanied by such an amnesiac trip, dangerous company when one is behind the wheel.

Only my arm, with the skin darkened by the blood under the dermis and the wound produced by the IV inserted, gave me back the taste of the memory of my short but intense relationship with Bergamo.

Suddenly Maria, my wife, arrived. Well, my fiancée, we were going to get married in December of that same year. But after many years together and two perfect but very naughty children, for me she was already my woman, my partner, my wife.

I looked over and in her left hand, she was holding a paper bag, from the local pharmacy in the small town where we lived.

My gaze became that of my children on Christmas morning, with that uncontrollable urge to open the presents and discover what was inside.

Incidentally, that day, after everything that had happened, they went to spend the day at their grandparents' house.

Quim, the eldest, and Nil lived

oblivious to my violent struggle and that's how it should remain, at least for the moment, they were too young to understand why their now useless father was incapable of holding them in his arms imagining they were paper aeroplanes as he had done until recently, that feeling, a grief that seemed to flood everything, was worse and more destructive than any pain.

He missed them very much, but he also longed for a good shot to try to alleviate, in part, that incomprehensible and undeserved pain,

I needed some pharmacological narcotic to turn me back into who I used to be.

I wanted drugs and I wanted them now, it wasn't addiction, I really needed them.

I suppose that, to feel perpetual and

horrendous pain and that thanks to certain substances, it fades away, creates a certain dependency.
So like a child, rummaging through his bag of Halloween candy, I desperately searched for my prize, my treat full of chemistry and pleasure.TRICK OR TREAT!!!! I kept repeating to myself.

I wanted the jackpot and I wanted it now.
Maria understood my need and left me alone with my little paper bag, I was about to start my well-deserved party. From my magic bag of sweets I took out three boxes, some anti-inflammatories that I couldn't remember the name of and that I wasn't particularly excited about and finally a bit of fun, the last two boxes contained the candy that all children want on the night of the thirty-first of October, opiates and fentanyl patches.

My eyes widened, I had my treats, my ticket to the magical and sparkling world of 'Wonderland'.
I had the tools to lead the way and the resources to fight like a man, against my central nervous system.
It was the first time I smiled, it was the first time I looked into the eyes of my beloved arthrosis and, maddened by the euphoria, by the pain suffered in the previous hours, thinking that soon I would give them a smile.
thinking that I would soon hunt them down, I quickly gave myself the medicines.
I had an insatiable appetite, I wanted to feel better and for that hell to be less burning and kinder.
But I soon underestimated the destructive power of my arthrosis and how fast the drugs can be.
After a few moments and with my pupils already dilated from the mixture

of fentanyl and opium coursing through my veins and I could feel them inside, a feeling of bravery, running down my back, I tried to get up.
Inside my head I glimpsed and imagined that it would be a heroic and epic act, I was going to emulate President Roosevelt himself, or so I thought, I was going to stand up and say that....;
Don't say it can't be done. Nothing is impossible.
But when I was beginning to glimpse, to touch the summit, to nail the flag and rise over that epic, impracticable six-foot mountain, to finally, at last, be able to stand up. I felt something push me against the bed, it was like falling off a cliff, with no ropes or ledges to hold on to, I went from being Roosevelt to emulating poor Judy Garland being

abused by the vicious dwarves in the Wizard of Oz, lying helpless on that bed.

I became sweet, helpless Dorothy Gale forced backstage, suffering the onslaught of the Munchkins, while the tin man played a voyeur, groping himself.

When I tried to get out of it, something pushed me again, falling on the same bed and not letting me move or get up, even the damned lion of the world of Oz, who was no longer a coward, was also encouraged to participate in my innocent sweetness.

That bunch of pimps, whores, and hustlers infested my room.

It was a party, but not how I imagined it or how I wanted it to be, I was the main course of the evening, there was no truce or treat, only the tricks of those damned knaves.

I became a rag doll, unable to stand up.

CHAPTER V
Enola Gay

I woke up after a few moments or so I thought... the cuckoo clock I had in the room, unstoppable and totally apathetic to what had happened, showed me like a punch in the face, that hours had passed since the insatiable feast I enjoyed and the characters of the Wizard of Oz paid homage to each other.

I thought I remembered, that between my legs they passed one after the other and after their feast they tried to smother me against the pillow.

For me, it was all very clear, a product of my imagination, invaded by prescription psychotropics, or maybe

not, maybe they were there with me, I think I was going crazy.
There I was, lying between the sheets, with the infinite white that adorned all the walls of the room. Only the pleasant orange light of the sunset, the mentally healing scent of lavender coming through the window and the cuckoo clock helped me understand what time of day it was and helped me forget what had happened.
After a while, suddenly and without warning, the taste of dry cork took over my entire gullet. For the first time in twenty-four hours I was thirsty and that was bad.
The distance that separated me from the nearest water source was almost insurmountable,

'alea iacta est.

I was about to embark on a

treacherous journey in search of water.

Life seemed too hard for such a small mammal, it wasn't a huge distance, but those eight metres of cracks in the ground, separating me from the kitchen, seemed exacerbated.
I got back on the bed with extreme caution, turned around, placed one foot and then the other on the floor. With the help of a blue cane that had become my binomial since that day although I never knew how it got there, I was able to get up.
Meter by meter, step by step, eight steps out and eight steps back in total, I had to at least try. The thirst was so strong that it was worth risking my life for a few drops of water to put in my mouth.
Each step was tormenting; bolts digging into my bones, drilling, drilling and drilling in life, without

anaesthesia. All that suffering was had to be necessary?

Halfway through, I stopped for a moment, leaning a trembling hand against the wall, trying to steady myself, as the pain burned every fibre of my body.

My slow, shuffling footsteps echoed in a house that was too silent. Every metre a victory.

But at last, I reached the kitchen, the tap seemed far away, but I reached it with my hands, clinging to the kitchen top as my last source of support. As I turned on the tap, the sound of the water flowing in a cool, running stream was a temporary relief, but unable to fight the pain.

It was unbelievable that such a simple act for me was a victory.

I felt I had found a shining fountain in the middle of the empty, burning desert.

A bloody oasis in the middle of the house.

That journey made me think about the journeys that the women of some tribes in Guinea Bissau have to make in search of water. How brave they are.

I had a few good, well-deserved drinks before I made my way back home, back to my bed.

Only there I felt moderately well, although accompanied by a pain that tormented me, sticky and unpleasant company.

In this life, the only thing to be afraid of is fear itself, and the only thing that made me panic was the pain itself, the one I felt constantly, I was sick of living in that habitat and of being unable to get out of it, as if trapped in a thick jungle where danger lurks in every corner.

But even on dry land, in a jungle like

that, where it seems that nothing worse can or should happen, disasters do happen.

Once I reached my goal, I set my stick against the wall and as best I could, I threw myself on the bed, my mouth and throat are now satiated.

Suddenly a quick spiral of intense dry pain and emptiness settled in my battered hip.

On August 6, 1945, during the final stages of World War II, the Enola Gay became the first plane to drop an atomic bomb, the Little Boy, which fell on the Japanese city of Hiroshima and almost completely obliterated it, leaving behind nearly seventy thousand dead bodies and tens of thousands more as a result of the radiation.

My hip became that Japanese city. Without warning, cowardly and from behind, a burning, indescribable pain began to emerge almost out of nowhere, with malice aforethought and extreme cowardice.

Choking on my own oxygen, I tried to gasp for air but was unable to oxygenate my lungs. The pain was so searing that I was drowning even though I was full of fresh air.

It was like being underwater, but on dry land.

As best I could, I looked back at my hip and its deformed anatomy, staring at it in astonishment, panic in my eyes, living the situation that no one ever expects to live through.

That 1945 B-29 Superfortress had crashed on my left side, fully loaded with the radioactive poison on board.

I didn't even want to look, I didn't even dare to look, I couldn't fill my lungs with air.

It was a horrible sensation, as if I had found a tree blackened by some

ancient fire that had turned the colour of charcoal and from it hung a body, a hanged man. I...
At that moment I didn't want to die, but I didn't want to live either.
A mixture of conflicting feelings that reminded me of my insatiable need to feel the effects of narcotics.
Again.
Sweet nightmares, horrible lucidity.

CHAPTER VI
Steaming Horses

I held my breath so that I could squirm and discover more consciously, the deformity I had acquired in my hip.

Its shape reminded me of Chernobyl's reactor number four on the night of 26 April 1986, on the verge of a core meltdown, about to explode, in that corner of Ukraine.

Everything pointed to the fact that it was time to embark on a new psychotic journey.

Everything pointed to the fact that he had to open the drawer of delights, again, and rummage, by touch alone, for opioids and fentanyl.

Every second that passed was a horrendous and painful death, I had to look for them and I had to find them fast.

Only with the help of my hands, since moving a single centimetre of my lower body, battered on the bed, would turn into kilometres of suffering in a burning desert with no supplies.

At last and without hesitation, when I touched them, I grabbed the two boxes of my delicious and necessary drugs.

Already my forehead was already wetting drop by drop with a cold sweat, caused by addiction or fever... it didn't matter.

So, I swallowed the opium, hooked the patch of sweet fentanyl on my slippery skin.

Soon and again, dilated pupils.

The drugs, like steaming horses, were already coursing through my veins,

sailing at full sail, using my blood like a sea.
I felt my body rippling over the waves. Waves that died in a bay, but instead of taking me to the shore of a paradisiacal beach, they dragged me with their current towards a deep and immense dark blue, very dark ocean.

GOOD WIND AND GOOD SEA!!!!

My bed turned into a boat, took me towards what seemed to be the centre of an ocean, a sort of Nemo point, with no land in sight.
Suddenly, a few moments after setting sail, the waves were getting louder and louder.
Accompanied only by a lantern that danced to the sound of the waves, fed by oil, as best I could and with my cap on, as captain, I sailed on that sea.
The salty water of that ocean was

hitting the hull of my small boat harder and harder, and I had to hold on to my rudder to avoid falling overboard.

Wave on the port tack!!!!

That big swell announced to me that the storm had arrived.
The drops began to fall, the lightning flashes illuminated that lonely sea for tenths of a second and followed by that fleeting light, the sound of thunder.
I had never felt them so clearly, never heard them so close.
Millions of drops fell, one after the other, flooding everything,
leaving me soaked and without the company of the light of the lantern, killed by the rain, while, as best I could, I tried to defend myself from that endless storm with the help of my

little rudder.

Suddenly the water around and under my boat began to bubble and after that effervescence a whale appeared, it was enormous, it didn't seem to be less than fifteen metres long, for a moment I thought it was coming to laugh at me, to make that ocean journey more complicated, to be the only spectator of my demise.

But Oiken, the name by which I nicknamed her, seemed strangely friendly. She seemed to be fighting alongside my ship, battling the rough seas and the aggressive storm.

I had to take advantage of this improvised company, at least I was no longer alone in that immense oceanic void.

We fought shoulder to shoulder, facing the unleashed fury of the sea, deafened by the roar of the waves, which seemed to want to drag us into

the abyss. Oiken the whale was like
me, in the sense of fighting against
the sea, the storm was so powerful,
the swell so destructive that it didn't
seem the natural habitat for a whale
like that, and evidently, neither did
mine.
Our bodies tensed with each
onslaught, muscles burning to
maintain balance in the midst of the
chaos.
I looked to Oiken, with his steady
stance, his swim and his focused gaze,
he gave me the strength to keep
going. I could feel the struggle, his
body and mine, resisting every stroke
of the tide, backing out was not an
option and we both knew it.
The water pulled us, pushed us again
and again, with an unbridled rage, a
titanic struggle against the current, we
moved as one being, synchronised by

the need to survive, fighting for a nature that did not want to give in.

My improvised friend and I surfed on the salty water for a long time, I was not aware of how long, but the drops, the fight against the swell and the thunder seemed to me like a clock stopped in time, each thunder preceded by lightning second by second, drop by drop.
We fought against wind and tide, reefs that shattered hulls and beloved Oiken skin.
From time to time he expelled air and droplets through his blowhole, as if to try to return to the sky, droplets that fell from thick clouds without any resistance and thus compensate for such savage weather.
We sailed together for a long time, chasing a horizon that didn't seem to get closer, further and further away

from it, more and more impossible, it
was as if we were moving away every
time we approached it, like an absurd
and senseless loop, until suddenly:
Oiken, my beloved whale, stood still
for a moment, floating on the surface
of the water as if time did not exist.
His eyes, dark and deep, looked at me
one last time, full of a silent wisdom
that seemed to say what words were
unable to be explained.
With a slow, majestic movement,
Oiken began to descend. His massive
body, which for so long had been my
strength, dipped with an elegance that
contrasted with his imposing size.
The water closed over him, swallowing
his silhouette bit by bit, silent farewell,
immediate emptiness.

Farewell Oiken.

After what seemed like endless hours,

now alone and without the company of my favourite whale, that powerful squall began to subside and on those already weakened clouds, small stars began to appear in that night sky, on that dark ceiling, it seemed as if the drops had stopped, no longer falling, suspended in the air.

It took me a few moments to realise that they were not drops, but the cosmos with its constellations, over the open sky.

There were no more clouds.

Guided by the stars, by my contracted experience that I had acquired during those hours, together with Oiken and as a ship's captain, I began to sail in pursuit of the big bear.

With the sleeve of my 'Pea Coat' I wiped the moisture from my forehead, produced by the rain, and from its pocket, I took an compass to guide me.

With the swell the water becoming calmer, my boat along rippled pleasantly, almost sedately, as my dogged perseverance seemed almost obsessed with chasing the brightest light of the mainsail.

Once reconstituted from the exhaustion of that storm, I sailed over the sea, caressing the waves, the breeze drying my forehead and my sailor's clothes.

With the mainsail fully hoisted, my boat seemed to lose contact with the sea water.

Faster and faster, my little vessel did the impossible, or maybe not, a powerful gust of wind seemed to fly my boat.

With that eagerness to chase that star, it took flight, I looked overboard, it was five, ten, fifteen metres above the sea, higher and higher.

The big bear started to grow, or maybe I was getting closer by the minute.

It seemed impossible that this was happening, I almost felt it was possible to touch it with my hands.

So I continued on my brave expedition into the infinity of the cosmos.

Getting bigger and bigger, more and more bearish, I was getting so close, it was huge.

It was so close, that my whole range of vision was almost blinded by that pure white, almost divine. Everything was candid. It seemed almost as if it was a mighty dawn.

And suddenly as I was caressing it with my fingertips, everything became like the ceiling and walls of the room, dazzling, where I was recovering from my fucking hip and where the cuckoo clock, began to chime announcing the arrival of a new day.

The storm ceased, the swell became
sheets and my boat became a bed.
I was back in safe harbour, tired and
frightened, but in harbour at last, the
cuckoo clock stopped chiming,
everything returned to the same old
normality, in a strange way, I longed
for Oiken.
After a while, when my bed no longer
rippled with the tide, I tried to make
sense of what had happened.
I didn't fully understand the situation I
had just experienced. That star, that
whale, that lantern moving to the
sound of my boat, drenched in rain,
that epic adventure.
No matter how hard I tried, I couldn't
make sense of what I had
experienced, as always, the guilt, the
medication, but?
To what extent?
Each situation experienced, each
struggle, each drop of blood spilled,

each time seemed more real than the
last.

CHAPTER VII
An Angel in the Rain

I did not understand what had just happened, my bed was suddenly once again moored to the floor of my room, to that harbour from which it did not seem to have moved.

My odyssey across the ocean appeared, as if it had only been a dream, too real to be fiction, too fantastic to be real.

What I experienced seemed to be the result of taking the drugs, but as I say, I felt it, I lived it, every moment as if it were really authentic, with my forehead still wet.

Every time I took one of those little

shiny pills, or the fentanyl stuck to my skin, something happened in my head. I started to become both afraid of them and addicted to them.
It wasn't normal what was happening to me, when the drugs started to take effect and I was terrified, but at the same time, I longed to see what was behind the door of the rainbow they made me travel to.
In any case, those sedative, hallucinogenic substances made me escape from pain for what seemed like a few hours a day, and even if I embarked on countless dangers and adventures, they were necessary.
It was worth the risk.
I could not continue to dwell on it, it was almost noon.
Since I could hardly stand up, I had not been able to take a well-deserved shower or shave for days, and that afternoon my doctor was coming to

visit me.

Our little surgery was close to home, no more than a five-minute walk away, but fetching water, inside my house, was an obscene odyssey, taking into account my obligatory rest; the doctor visited me at home frequently to check on my condition and evolution.

I was grateful for that.

So, with the help of my cane, I was able to stand up.

Clumsy and extremely bent over, I managed to reach the bathroom, one hand on the cane, the other on the wall.

Even with the help of the crutch and the walls, my movement was very orthopaedic and painful.

Sitting down was painful and lifting my leg to get into the shiny white bathtub was even more so....

Luckily some soul, some ghost, with extreme stealth, had installed one of those grab rails. I used them without hesitation and they helped me complete my task.

Thank you.

So after several days trapped in discomfort and pain, I allowed myself the luxury of taking a shower.

Inside the bathtub and with extreme caution, I had crossed the point of no return. I turned on the tap, the sound of falling water filled the bathroom and when the first warm drop touched my skin, a sigh of relief washed over me. Warm, comforting water, sliding over my body, taking some of the pain with it.

Being able to wash myself, even in pain, did more than anyone could imagine, I didn't understand how that simple act, flooded me with the will to live.

With my cheeks flushed by the hot water, I understood that every drop of water is life.

Never waste it, reader.

When I finally turned off the tap, the cool air of the bathroom contrasted with the warmth still lingering in my body. I reached for my towel, soft and fluffy to the touch, and carefully ran it over me. Its texture, so cosy, could be felt as delicate caresses, drying the water, but leaving a sense of relief, letting its comfort, enveloping me completely, as if the towel embraced me after days of storm. After that, I returned to my bedroom.

That act was so pleasant, that nature wanted to get infected, looking out of the window, I saw that it had started to rain heavily.

It seemed like one of those late summer storms, soaking and refreshing the whole atmosphere, although very noisy and with a violent wind.

The next few minutes passed
normally, while the trees swayed in
the wind and the rain left everything
wet in its path, I turned on the
television I had in the room, to distract
myself for a while, although as usual,
the news channel was not too hopeful,
they were talking about the typical
tension between countries with
nuclear capacity. In the meantime, I
was waiting for the doctor's visit,
which was not long in coming.
I heard someone knocking on the door
of the house and then the sound of the
front door opening and from the room
I heard the murmur of two people
greeting each other and the heavy
rain behind the entrance.
The door emitted a peculiar sound,
which warned me of each arrival even
if I didn't hear the bell, as it squeaked
a little when someone opened it, how
many times I told myself that I should

grease it, I should never leave anything for later, maybe tomorrow it will be impossible to do it.

...I memorized this, at that moment.

A few seconds later, an angel appeared in my room, wearing a white coat, slightly dampened by the rain, really shining. It was my doctor with the typical stethoscope hanging behind her neck.
After the initial conversation we had to bring the doctor up to date on my discomfort, and then, she proceeded to inject my sore hip with cortisone and reminded me that hopefully I would soon be operated on. We knew each other well, our doctor cared for the health of my family. I understood that's why the visit was so fleeting, she was probably surprised and upset to see me in that state,

especially knowing my medical history.
Empty for a lifetime and full of
ailments and pain in just one night.
She told me that it would take a
couple of days to take effect and that I
should rest as much as possible,
I thought I would have no problems, as
I could hardly walk.
I didn't think at the time to tell him
about the trips I went on every time I
took my medication, I didn't think
anything of it.

CHAPTER VIII
Dark and infinite

It was some time since the doctor had closed the door on her way out. I remained as usual lying in bed.

It was difficult to try to pass the time in this state, a bit of television, maybe the daily newspaper, or even write a novelistic diary, in case someone in my same situation, or maybe for the pleasure of reading, wants to enter into this crazy story I'm going through. In any case, my greatest pastime was looking out of the window, and that's just what I was doing at that very moment.

The sun, behind the clouds, was setting with strange slowness. It seemed that it didn't want to go to sleep that day, or maybe that was the feeling it gave me, as it was still hidden behind the strong storm.
The sky, very cloudy, was the typical orange-grey colour of the typical summer rains. Although the beautiful picture didn't last long, it looked as if someone very talented had drawn a beautiful stormy sky with watercolour on a canvas.
My wife, always attentive, brought me something for dinner, on the typical tray that is placed on the bed to bring breakfast and flowers to your loved one, or so that an unfortunate sufferer of osteoarthritis could fill his listless belly with some nourishment.
The previous days I could not eat anything at all, I only drank water and the truth is that it made me lose a few

extra kilos.

After a small dinner, it was time to collect the flight tickets and cross the security cordon again, I opened the medicine box, I was sure that I was going to embark on a new hallucinogenic adventure and unfortunately, nothing good was about to happen.

I had already studied the size of my pupils, but even so, I was unable to get my eyes used to the darkness. How does an eye get used to fear...? I asked myself.

It was already dark, when I suddenly tried to turn on the lamp on the desk next to me so as not to sink into complete shadow.

I couldn't find the little table, nor the drawer. My hand came up against what looked like a wall, close, very close. Barely ten centimetres separated me from that impossible

barrier.
I turned around and came up against the evil twin of the wall, that a moment before I had touched with my hand just on the other side.
It was shrouded in darkness, suffocating; The air began to thicken, barely passing my lips, each breath shorter than the last.

WHAT THE FUCK IS GOING ON?

When I tried to sit up, a crack in my hips followed by a blow on my forehead, one of those that shows you that the path is wrong, again another malevolent wall, this time, a ceiling above me, equal to ten centimetres.
I understood absolutely nothing, I was inside what looked like a damn box and from the feel of it, it wasn't good news.
My head quickly went into the worst

possible situation, maybe I had suffered a catalepsy and had been buried alive, I couldn't remember how I had got into such a situation.
Shit, shit, think, think fast, fuck, I told myself... I was looking for a useless way to get out of that fucking mousetrap with no way out, without the fucking cheese as a prize for having solved the labyrinth.
Maybe I was dead, or worse, maybe I was still alive.
Yes, I was, I was still fucking alive and that was worse than anything that had ever fucking happened to me before.
Strangely,the mobile phone I'm writing right now, appeared in my hand, buried in life, it didn't even have coverage, the typical 'X' logo appeared accompanied by a 'no signal'.
The terror that people suffer for not being able to send a message on time

and for me, this means that I am
slowly approaching a pitiful, agonising
and mute death because no matter
how much I shrieked no one seemed
to hear me.

The weight of the earth, on me,
became more oppressive with every
second. I could feel pressure on my
chest, preventing me from inhaling air
completely, I was choking.

So, that's why I'm writing these lines
for say goodbye, so that if one day you
dig me up next to my wretched mobile
phone, you will know why.

YOU BASTARDS BURIED ME ALIVE!!!!!

I sobbed... while little by little, the CO2
began to vitiate the atmosphere so I
resigned myself to having a sweet
death, without agony, I almost
expected it, I loved it like the loved
one you wait for at the airport next to

the arrivals gate, or to know how to turn around without anyone to say goodbye to me at the departure gates. Everything was so dark, it was beautiful, as if someone lost sight of the horizon and the world ended an inch away. It was like looking at something close and infinite at the same time.

I closed my eyes to try to travel another time, another moment in my life.

But the effort was in vain, because the human being, even when travelling through time, can only do so at a constant and unmovable speed of one second per second.

When the tent had almost embraced me and I was ready to let myself be seduced by its cold and rough skin... the light appeared, again. Again, the shutter of my room opened suddenly, putting an end to what; God knows what had happened to me, a bad dream or again an out-of-body experience produced by my beloved hallucinogens.

In any case, not knowing how, a new day was born, just like me.

Was it all caused by my treacherous medicines or maybe not?

The important thing at that moment was that I could breathe again with apparent normality, but everything seemed to me, that I had, experienced it with extreme reality.

CHAPTER IX
Harvests of Peace

Hours gave way to days, and days to weeks. It's something we all know and use as time travel when, in between, we have nothing better to explain than silence.

Looking out of the window, the picture was already autumny, from my room.I could see the garden and there suddenly, playing oblivious to my gaze, were two small and foolish birds, my children, appeared.

It seemed incredible but while I was in my unpleasant incapacity, unable to move, I hadn't noticed how fast Quim and Nil had grown up.

I realised that children grow

independently of us, no matter how we are, they are like fruit trees, which we see growing season by season, but not during the year, no matter how much we look at them constantly.
They grow without asking permission from life, in an act of organic obedience, and civil disobedience, for they were quite naughty, like all children.
Watching them playing in the garden I realised, with incredible naturalness, like reckless birds, that these nappyless creatures were growing up.
I missed them so much inst lately. I only saw them on their fleeting visits to my room, but like the children they are, they were short and impatient visits, like birds that come for a crumb of bread and then fly away.
As I looked out of the window, I thought that I should have gone more to their bedside, in the evenings, not

rushing to put them to sleep, but above all to listen to their souls breathing conversations of words and meaningless confidences between sheets and pillow.

That day I learned that the possibility of bathing them, putting them to bed, were not exhausting tasks without patience at the end of the day, they were opportunities to smell them, to hug them, to listen to them; They were not chores,

They were acts of unconditional love, They were opportunities to create new memories in them.

That day I learned that I only had one dream. I didn't want them to grow up without having used up every last drop of my affection for them. I learned to want to see them grow day after day, night after night.

Watching Quim and Nil grow up was a whirlwind of deep emotions.

Every struggle they faced, whether in the daylight or in the stillness of the night, forged in them a unique strength.

It was like watching the creation of beings still incomplete, but full of potential. Their differences, their challenges and their victories, went hand in hand in a shared journey, that even knowing that their path was yet to be defined, they were already able to show me the horizon with the strength and confidence of a giant.

CHAPTER X
Hooks

Shortly lasted that apparent tranquillity, with which, oblivious to everything that was happening, my children regaled me from the window.
Suddenly, and without making any strange gesture, a stabbing pain began to run through my left leg, above all I felt the pain in the left big to of the foot.
It was like a pain caused by uric acid, an attack of gout so to speak.
but the reality was going to be worse. Peripheral neuropathy crossed the path, along with osteoarthritis. As if it were love at first sight, these two ailments fell in love and began to

travel together.

This toxic, painful and disgusting friendship emerged out of nowhere. It was truly horrible. It was no longer embers or crystals, it was Wes Craven's most perverse fantasy. A nervous highway, which my leg had become, with hundreds of vehicles crashing into each other senselessly, creating a jumble of iron, salt and rust and me in the middle of all that metal ball.

I felt every nervous impulse as if someone was burning me with a cigarette.

I tried to stand up, but not even with the help of my beloved blue crutch could I take a step.

It was like having a fishhook stuck in my bunion bone. But the fishing line was taut and not made of nylon, I couldn't pull it out. My big toe became the bait.

The more I pulled, the more it got stuck.

It was nauseating, I gave up and lay back on the bed as best I could. I could smell the putrid, metallic odour of the old, decaying hook, stuck in my bone.

Mentally I couldn't take it anymore, I was already mortally wounded, in a slow and painful demise. It was an open and purulent mass to which added was a cut over an open wound. The straw that broke the camel's back. My bones felt shattered, as if that pain, added to the pain in my hip, had liquidised my bone mass, like a cavity in my foot.

I will never find an adjective that does justice to that evil, but it was as if my nerves through my spinal cord, as an emissary, always brought bad news. News like November 22nd, sixty-three. It was half past twelve noon and I became Harvey Oswald's target and that bullet was meant for me.

With the difference that the value of my life, at that instant, seemed to be less than the price of that damned bullet in the temple.

I grabbed the phone as if it were a weapon, to defend myself from such a petty aggression, I called my doctor who came quickly, to confirm what I already knew was happening to me. Luckily she brought some medicine to try and stop the hollow, stabbing pain. Again she was like an angel and although her efforts were admirable and helped keep me alive, my breath was far from dignified.

I really felt like a constrictor snake was squeezing my neck, my life had been turned upside down, from leading a normal life like most....

I went from that, to being gathered at

the Spahn ranch and I would have
taken on the role of Sharon Tate.

CHAPTER XI
Retail Trade

After talking to my doctor then a second visit, it dawned on me that I hadn't been to work for a few months now.

And my phone hadn't rung in all that time, not one measly message.

So, filled with that uneasiness and a kind of

of inspiration that ran through my body, I took a sheet of paper and my favourite pen from my desk.

I used, as I always do when I have to write, a white offset paper.

I was part of a multinational company dedicated to telecommunications and it is wrong for me to say it, but despite being a number like everyone else in a

large company, I was not just one of them.
Considered one of the most sought-after salesmen of the last decade, where every day I received praise, invited to events and possibly one of the most influential motivational speakers of recent times. Despite all this, it was as if my being ill had erased me from that exclusive list. I was no longer invited to the party.
But one thing was clear to me: if my phone didn't ring while I was fighting, it wouldn't answer when I won.
Although it pissed me off that I had not been treated as an investment and that is usually the biggest problem, an employee should be treated as an investment, not as an expense.
Expenses fuck and at that moment I was fucking more than one.
My boss, despite having arthrosis like me and empathising before I went on

sick leave, seemed concerned about
my health before I fell ill.
I thought it was a real concern, but the
phone, again, didn't ring, never rang,
never broke the silence of my rest.
But if you ever read this, I want you to
know that I would have loved to have
my phone ring.
That you would have told me that
arthrosis has not understood how
strong life is, that it is a cowardly and
senseless disease, that it makes you
bleed and wins rounds, but that it is
never a winner, if you had done so... I
would never have doubted you.
You always bragged about our
friendship, you showed me off like a
trophy to be taken care of and now
your finger points at the back of my
head, like the one that points at the
sick or the enemy.
But you never decided to call, to wish
for a speedy recovery, for me, for you,

out of simple humanity.
Your old trophy is now struggling, caked in dust, but struggling to shine again.
Someday I will point the finger at you, but in your eyes and in your face. I will tell you what you never made me hear and what I so desperately needed to hear, I will explain to you that our illness has no reason, that you will get over it, or maybe not.
But be sure that it will be a hard battle, a war without ammunition, without troops and with only one weapon, bravery.

Dear boss, osteoarthritis is a disease, it lacks feelings, it perishes in the face of courage, but it kills cowards.
Remember that the day your phone doesn't ring, remember that... silence sometimes kills innocents.
This chapter was important, but you

don't deserve to benefit from the only thing that can never be recovered, life, time, and just as bees don't waste time explaining to flies, because honey is better than shit, I don't intend to waste it with you anymore.
So use this writing whenever you need it.
Sincerely, your dusty trophy.
Next, I folded the sheet designed and dressed in dark blue letters, safeguarded it inside an envelope and adorned it with a commemorative postage stamp majestically depicting the Red Wall of Calp and left it for mailing, finally noting the return address and addressee.
The next day, the envelope and its powerful contents disappeared from the little table where I put it to rest after having written it.
I really think that I will never regret having written that. I put spirit into

those miserable words witch I was
proud to have expressed in a letter
addressed to a superior all that and in
that way, with words that we could
never make come out live, but we are
masters of what we write.

I had no regrets...

CHAPTER XII
Second Circle

Popular belief says that hell is a place full of sinners, constantly burning, to atone for their sins.
constantly, to atone for their sins.
I was still alive in a hell, already tinged with white, Christmas was approaching and with it, the cold.
Last weeks rain was already falling in the form of persevering snow, I felt very lonely as I lost the company of some birds that I used to hear during the warmer months and some curious cats that came to the window from time to time.
The children no longer played on the greenish grass, already covered by

thick snow, nor did the crickets
provide my evenings with their
melodic songs.
There was only the cold in this climatic
winter, but it was so powerful that it
not only froze with its breath, streets
and homes, which with much effort,
kept the smoke coming out of their
chimneys constant.
Strangely, it penetrated muscles and
arteries, and I soon realised that what
I was feeling was not the drop in
temperature typical of the time of
year.
I missed my dear wife. With my
wasted hip, my medication and
everything else, it had been months
since we had any intimacy together.
we couldn't be a couple.
It was neither obsession nor vice, just
love, companionship and affection.
I missed her caresses, her hugs, I
missed her, I missed feeling us

together when the children slept.

It had been weeks since we had heard complicit laughter, or a glass of wine being filled, it had been months since our skin had felt togetherness for the last time.

There was nothing to celebrate.

I wanted her, but in that second circle of cold, wintry hell, I felt as if an arthritic impotence had taken me as its only lover.

I wanted her, but she, with more sense than me, answered in the negative.

I must admit that many times I thought that it was because I was a waste in that state, fragile and broken, or that I was no longer the virile male who, as if he were an orangutan, conquered his female one summer night, in the middle of the mating season, I couldn't blame her?

I was no longer that masculine being who once was young and slender and

moved like a feline. I had become the opposite.
Suddenly I was trapped in Dante's second circle, no sinner of lust, just enough. Virgil was already ordering Dante to condemn me unjustly for letting my carnal appetites overcome my reason.
Lust reigned and the air was filled with overflowing desires.
That hell, that senseless punishment, where I did not find myself in the company of Paris, Tristan or Helen of Troy.
Only men, women, ethereal figures around me, luring me, whispering false promises, faceless.
I had the sensation of being overwhelmingly harassed, feeling penetrated by non-existent limbs, seeking to possess me completely.
I tried to escape, but each step took

me deeper into the labyrinth of unbridled passions.

Capable of screaming, sinners of lust all of them, that they were punished there as I was, who tried to make my way through that crowd, while with their whispers, like siren songs, they tried to drag me to perdition, in an internal struggle of fear and desire. Those tenants of the second circle had learned nothing, they were thirsty for lust and sex and I was the novelty.
In the same way I discovered that punishment is quicker than the truth and for whatever reason, Dante did not trust me.
I could only hear between the simultaneously painful and pleasurable moans, which, without naked bodies to emit them, echoed off walls made of moistened female crotches, it was sickening and

tempting at the same time.
Walls that incited me to madness sinful cheating walls that tried by all means to get me close to them to gather flesh but no soul, there was no salvation in that place.
They were sweet, extremely sweet, I would even dare to say almost innocent, they urged me to let myself be seduced by pleasure, they whispered in my ear, they told me to take them time after time.
But I was stronger, I was more impotent.
I was alone, punished by a conquering cold and a violent wind, excitingly sexual and below zero, crashing against my body which, even with clothes on, seemed almost naked, or maybe really naked, because of the fear and insecurity of finding myself alone in that vicious second circle.
There was something about that place,

obscene and dirty, that provoked a kind of frozen excitement. There was nothing down there that attracted me, nor did I suffer from philias in my day to day life, but that darkness, that cold was hot.

I never considered myself lustful, but Dante punished me relentlessly, just for wanting to have sex, even with tired eyes, with my partner.

It wasn't lust, I simply loved my wife. I simply wanted her to hold me so tight, to bring my bones together again.

CHAPTER XIII
Enemy trench

The hours and days went by, we were in the middle of winter, through my beloved window, I could see the snow falling, the snow that brought me a little closer to the outside world, the first Christmas carols were already resounding, decorating and conquering, together with the typical smell of gingerbread biscuits, the festive atmosphere. We were only a few days away from Christmas.
I have to admit that these days have always been my favourite time of the year.
My doctor brought me a present in advance,

as during one of her visits, a few days before and with a new dose of cortisone, she had

cortisone, she made my life a little more worth living.

At least I could take a few steps without dying in the attempt, my doctor gave me the freedom to stand up and walk a few short distances with my beloved cane.

At the same time, she reminded me that we had to change our plans, as I was due to have my spine operated on before my hip.

The neuropathy, which had appeared out of nowhere weeks before, was gaining weight, almost pushing the osteoarthritis and the pelvic fracture into second place.

A truce, a ceasefire that negotiated life with arthrosis, at least for those days.

There we were on both sides, soldiers

dead with cold and fear, trying to
avoid as much as possible the freezing
temperatures under our trenches.
We didn't want to hear a shot, we
didn't want to feel the sound of
shrapnel, nor the light produced by
mortar fire on that dark, freezing
night, but we were on the lookout for
any ceasefire violations.
But all seemed very quiet, from the
other side of the battlefield, in the
enemy trench, a whisper began to be
heard, a melody of concord.
So after thinking about it, I grabbed a
white rag as a sign of surrender and
slowly approached to give a token of
peace, a present for those days and in
gratitude for that night of
togetherness.
I came out of my trench and after that,
I closed the door, little by little I
approached that enemy, converted in
that precious moment, into a friend

with an expiry date, so I had to take advantage of that moment of companionship.
Little by little the carols sounded louder and louder, encouraging me to go on. In the distance I glimpsed the silhouette of my wife and my two small children, at the beginning of the enemy trench, the street that nobody wants to tread.
Behind the door of the house, bloodthirsty soldiers, disguised in children's skins, on the enemy side and with red noses from the low temperatures, sang in a melodic voice, sang in a melodic voice a Christmas song, I can't remember which one.
On the way, I grabbed some sweets as a sign of friendship for hours.
I knew it would soon be over and my enemy would still be a traitor.

These creatures finished their concert
and I offered them this gift, they
accepted it gladly and slowly
disappeared into the mist, none of
them turned around in friendship,
none of them wanted peace, but
generals don't fight their own battles.
We were unknown soldiers, fighting
because someone decided we should.
Fake soldiers fighting, real battles, as
in all the wars that happen around the
world.
Politically incorrect, economically dirty
and authentically false,
because they all have the same thing
in common, they are signed in offices,
they are started in camps and on all
sides, the first victim is the truth.
It was just a business, a short
friendship for hours, which would soon
come to an end, they were on the
street, dangerous enemy territory.
And so they left, and I never saw those

brave fighters again, who were once powerful enemies who, holding destructive weapons, knew how to become friends.
The next day we would all return to our trenches and although my main enemy was my own body
my main enemy was my own body, I had to be clear about one thing,
the enemy of my enemy is still an enemy.
However much it may seem otherwise for a while, a few hours or a day, he is still the same impostor.

CHAPTER XIV
absurd and long

After that agreed truce, I returned to my base camp. I had to be calm, for in a few hours Iwas to be operated on, the surgeon was going to work his magic.

As the sun fled that day, the snow outside became thicker and thicker. It was one of the coldest winters I can remember. If not the coldest. As it was late and my loved ones were already asleep, I turned on the lamp on my bedside table, so that I could at least enjoy the company of the dim light it emitted.

It was an orange light, more for courtesy than to illuminate a large

room, and it flickered from time to time.
With the help of that company I took all my medicine..
Gradually the light grew dimmer, until I was plunged into deep darkness.
I tried to get my eyes used to the blackness, but I could only make out some long, faded shadows and what looked like a metal door.
An entrance that shouldn't be there, so I set out with the help of my mobile phone as a night viewer, with the brightness of the screen at maximum capacity and my crutch, I approached this absurd and impossible door.
It was extremely cold to the touch, I turned the knob that protected it from unauthorised opening and nothing happened.
I didn't understand why it had appeared almost out of nowhere, something so absurd.

I turned around and saw a few metres away a small almost infrared light and attracted like a moth in the dark, I approached it. When I reached that small luminescence, I could see that attached to that glow was a key, it was almost magical.

I quickly understood that I had to open that impossible metallic door, which had appeared out of nowhere in that place.

I turned around to cross my gaze again with that closed and inviolable entrance without the relevant authorisation.

The shadows became more and more pronounced and aggressive, caused by the glow of my mobile phone, but I couldn't be distracted by such monstrous apparitions, so I reached the door faster rather than slower, as I didn't trust those seemingly harmless shadows.

I inserted the key, which went in easily, almost as if the cylinder had been freshly oiled, turned the lock three times and the door opened, emitting a metallic, almost warning groan.

A sound to warn the unwary that such an entrance should not have been made open, not wanting to show what was hidden on the other side.

After sighing to make sense of that vision, that door to another world, my body passed through that entrance, I went to the other side, with a mixture of fear and curiosity.

What was clear to me was that if it had appeared there, with its metallic form, it must have been for a reason. I didn't know what the purpose was of this door leading to the unknown, but I wanted to find out. I entered, leaving the horrible, dense shadows behind me.

With the help of my phone I illuminated the room. Rather than a room, what appeared in front of me was an infinite corridor with such blackness that the brightness emitted by my mobile seemed to dim, a darkness seemed to absorb the light emitted. I then tried the torch that smartphones have nowadays.
It didn't do much good.
With my improvised torch and as if I had entered a cavern, I could recognise walls made of rough concrete and on both sides of the walls, with symmetrical distance between them, there were doors and more doors, exactly like the one I had crossed moments before, in my room, all cold, all made of metal.
That corridor, icy and dark, reminded me of a morgue, it was cold and gloomy. It was a place seized by terror,

I didn't even have the company of the typical crawling insect that nests in dark and damp places. In that place I was the only living being and the mist that arose from my breathing, warned me that I was still alive.

I began to walk,with my crutch, the clatter of each step I took echoed with a metallic sound and into the void, with no return.

The twin metal doors followed one after the other. It was so dark that even though I turned around to see the open door I had left behind, the one that could take me back to my room and leave me in a safe place, it seemed to have vanished. There was only darkness.

I swallowed my saliva trying to swallow something of value and continued forward.

Every step I took was like going deeper into the wolf's throat, I didn't want to be there, I shouldn't be there, despite the warning that the door to that dark corridor gave me. There was no light at all in that place, the silence, the darkness, was getting thicker and thicker.

An endless corridor ahead and nothing behind me. The long shadows that were produced in my room, seemed to have crossed that damned door, that and swallowed it, so it had acquired an impossible form and now they were chasing my steps.

I had no choice but to move forward, as the doors of that corridor appeared one,after another. Every step, every bloody metre I walked, I moved forward but they were so much the same that I seemed not to have moved from the same place.

I didn't think to open any of them at that time, maybe out of fear or because I was still trying to understand the impossible. Suddenly, a sharp sound violated the absolute silence.

My phone was complaining, already agonisingly warning me that its battery was running down, damn it.

I had no choice, faced with such warnings, but to try to escape from the hopeless, hopeless mousetrap as quickly as possible, I became a lab rat trapped in the middle of a failed experiment, the kind that shames the scientific community.

Desperate, I tried to open the first door I came across, but it was locked. It had no lock, no knob. It was as if someone had sealed it forever, after seeing inside, so that no unwary wretch would dare to open it again.

I continued.

With those menacing shadows, closer and closer, at my heels, and with the agony of not being able

to go through that narrow corridor
I tried a second door almost at
random. It was a gamble, die or be
killed, but nothing, impregnable.
For the moment I did not manage to
open any of the doors, I tried, looking
for a non-existent exit, that perhaps
did not exist but that any destination
they contained would be better than
escaping from those stalkers.
A second whine produced by the
telephone, warned me again that I was
running out of time. Soon I would be
submerged in an absolutely dark
madness.
I had to hurry as fast as I could, but
accompanied by interminable
slowness, it was like trying to run with
my shoelaces tied together. I couldn't
take steps of more than thirty
centimetres. Too far for a normal step,
too slow, too risky.
I knew that falling in that place or

trying to speed up my pace could make me stumble and leave me at the mercy and as the sole victim of the shadows that followed me there. That harassed me there, accompanied by another new fracture. I felt as if two wolves and a hen, locked up and with no way out, were deciding what they were going to have for dinner.
From time to time I turned to check the advantage I was losing by the moment, over the harassing shadows, but the glow of my mobile's torch, already dimmer due to the low battery, was unable to give me an approximation of the distance.
It was so dark that it seemed to swallow any glimpse of light, in that corridor, alone and as if the first door had become a black hole, sucking everything in, and by everything I mean even the hope of getting out of there alive.

They were too fast, I was too slow, and I was totally uninformed. Hidden news was not reaching me to give me any hope of getting out of there, in any possible way.

I was walking for metres and trying, without reward, to open identical doors until suddenly, a nightmare came true. The screen of my mobile, like a punch in the face, was printed on its screen, turning off in thirty seconds.

Just as, suddenly, my pain was joined by absolute blindness. I couldn't see anything. My phone had abandoned me and I had no other tools than my crutch. I took a step leaning my weight on it, to then use it as a cane for the blind. It was the only information I had at that moment, knowing that there was no obstacle in front of me.

I wasn't aware of the distance I had travelled and I wasn't willing to find out either, I couldn't take a single step backwards, I couldn't take a normal step forwards, without feeling that I would never reach the end.

Chills were starting to run down the back of my neck, I knew that the invisible was about to reach me. Suddenly, it caught me and my back as felt as if it were made of butter, a cold knife penetrating it, extremely sharp and burning at the same time. It was a painful sensation, very painful, it was cutting me, it was lacerating my skin with incredible ease. That damned shadow was stabbing me in the back, nightly, with extreme precision, time after time.

I felt it split my skin and flesh in two, in a deep, lacerating wound, piece by piece.

I could hardly move, nor howl, the pain was so deep that it choked before it left my mouth, I was alone in that place at the mercy of my dark aggressor. Too late that stabbing ceased without reason and extremely aggressive, but there was no relief, it seemed to release that butcher knife, to begin to mistreat me vertebra by vertebra, with what sensitively seemed a sledgehammer.

At thousands of blows per second, the pain coursed through my whole body. It was horrible, vomitous, so cruel that even my body was unable to exhale any steam from my insides, despite being badly wounded in that icy corridor.

I had become a kind of wooden plank, which they incessantly wanted to nail with screws, one after the other.

That shadow was killing me alive, in that corridor, unable to defend myself, I tried to move my limbs but they didn't respond,

She tried to call for help, but there was no sign of help and no one could hear her.

Once I was completely riveted, from one of the metallic doors appeared a kind of harpy, dressed like a seamstress. From one of the pockets of the dressing gown I was wearing, what looked like wool thread was peeping out, now that had become something totally horrifying, with precision and in my creepy immobility, she approached my beaten, cut and battered back.

With her hands he pulled my skin together and my flesh split in two, I could hear her almost whispering, it wasn't a sweet voice, it sounded more like a growl, her voice matched the pain I was feeling, I could never see or perceive her physique, except the two paws and her sharp fingers that peeked out from under his dressing gown, he pulled the ball of wool from her pocket and her darning needles and with microscopic precision, she began to sew me whole.

I could feel every twinge, piercing my back, feeling the rough thread entering through the hole caused by the sewing needle, I was suffering every stroke, horribly, penetrating her elongated needle into my

my bloody pulp.

I could smell the stench of blood and open wound, it was a foul stench, rotting flesh.

Standing, after a long time, leaning against a cold, rough, concrete wall, static and suffering from that morbid coven and with my pieces of flesh already sewn up, that tailor threw me unceremoniously against a kind of bed and took me away.

An unauthorised trip, gagged, towards one of the doors of that corridor,

and when she opened it a dazzling
white light came out of that room,
illuminating everything completely.
Dazzled I was left in that room when
suddenly another maid appeared, this
one did not grunt, this one did not
sew, she asked me how I was and with
my sickly and agonised voice, for all
that I had suffered in those endless
moments and with practically no
response from my moans, she asked
me how I was.
Trying to respond to the orders of my
mouth, I answered;
Kill me...
As I was practically unable to utter any
eloquent sound, he brought me a
sheet of paper and a marker pen.
Stupefied I stared and almost horrified
I looked at the sheet of paper which I
adorned with pain.
Well, on it and with a trembling pulse I

wrote; The anaesthetic has not worked, pain ten out of ten...

CHAPTER XV
Mummy

With my body still crucified, I was taken upstairs. The pain was endured thanks to the drip connected to one of my veins. Drop by drop that lotion was entering my bloodstream, leaving me levitating, almost ecstatic.

It was like living on the threshold between life and the end, with one foot in each world.

I would have loved death to have caught me, surrounded by friends and loved ones.

But at that moment I didn't need so much company. The orderly piloted me with the utmost caution into what was to be my temporary room.

It wasn't a bad place, relatively comfortable and solitary, wich is what I needed at that moment.
They say that if not for the better, silence is the best conversation one can have and I was able to have a good few hours to meditate on what had happened, in silence, talking to myself, with mute words.
The tedium was interrupted by the first visitor I had in that all-inclusive room, my dear mother.
A being who shone brightly, who was always there.
She was a person willing to sacrifice herself whenever necessary, I still remember when she warned me that life was going to strike, that it was not going to be easy, but that in case of maximum need she would be able to amputate a limb if her litter needed it.
As I would do if necessary for my own.
But this struggle I was living, was mine

alone, my mother could pave the way, but when destruction shakes the whole world at every step, not even the most powerful super heroine can handle it all. My mother didn't need powers to be necessary, just her presence there, without a word was more than enough, able to bring forth life using silence.

She sacrificed her whole life and gave me the wisdom of a father and the gentleness of a mother.

She had made me into the man I am today, still in the making, with the first feathers sprouting from my back, to end up as wings.

That is what my mother gave me, wings to fly as high as she could not and always wanted to.

But your effort will not be in vain.

When you find stones along the way, build; if you find holes use them to accumulate water, food and when life hits you, which it will do without mercy, get up using wings.

She taught me that the good thing about feeling pain is that even if you think it is eternal, it is always temporary. Everything happens for a reason.

And although she couldn't save me from that agonising suffering, only with silence she knew how to make me feel better.

She was my mother, the person who gave me life, the person who lent me her wings so that I could take flight, while she fell into an abyss for the simple fact of seeing her son in that situation.

That was my mother, a compassionate being who knew how to give me the best of all worlds, who taught me that life would strike, who taught me how to be a good parent.

CHAPTER XVI
Admission and Return

The days at the hospital, of admission to that all-inclusive resort, passed relatively quickly. Although it was a monotonous succession of hours and minutes, and the only recreational activities proposed were those of blood tests, breakfast, lunch, dinner and changing the IV several times a day. Every now and then I had the occasional visit from someone who, absent-mindedly, opened the door by mistake, thinking that they would find a loved one inside, not a stranger.

I felt an uneasy relative tranquillity. The hospitality of the place was to be appreciated and the painkillers to be enjoyed.

The first night in the hospital was the worst. My guts growled outrageously, demanding a ration to put in my mouth. But the rationing was severe and non-negotiable.

I hadn't had my molars to work, nor my throat to swallow, since eight in the morning that day and when I looked at the clock, we were about to cross the line, the threshold that separates the days.

Despite this, I survived, and when the food arrived, despite being cadaverous, I ate it. It was the typical hospital tray with some lettuce and a fish that had lived through better times and perhaps would have preferred to end its days on the counter and in front of the knife of a good chef.

But there it was, cooked in its worst

version, hot on the outside, raw and almost frozen on the inside.

I remember how I struggled to chew it, how I struggled to swallow it, even if I tried to give it the end it deserved, it clung to my throat causing me a stabbing pain, but it wasn't the fault of that fish speared between my jaws. That affliction was caused by the injury, of the tube inserted in my windpipe to keep me alive during the butchery.

Sleep and painkillers were more powerful than hunger, I slept peacefully and after that fierce battle lost against by that powerful fish, I left it alone to rest in peace.

The next day, I had the most awaited visit of all. My eyes opened at the same time as the door and there, my two little innocent birds. For them their father was still a hero. I still remember Quim, asking me while he looked stupefied at my skin connected to drippers, cables and lines, if what they were doing in that hospital was turning people into robots.

I did indeed answer yes.
Nil asked me when I would sleep with them again.
Maria who came, together with the children's grandmother, looked at me, my eyes moistened by my tears. We both understood a lot with very little. The father of my children was not a loser, a wreck... He was a flying robot who would soon return to sleep with them.
The next three days in hospital passed relatively quickly with the clock ticking inexorably, so after the needle had turned seventy-two times, I was given the 'check out' paper and I was eager to return to my homeland, to my home.

With extreme caution, I went through the majestic door of that hospital centre, I had to be careful as the snow at that time had turned to ice and I did not have the means to survive a slide or a fall. With what seemed like slow and steady steps, I arrived at the 'check point', the small vehicle that my wife used to drive.

I don't remember what the trip to the hospital to have the operation was like, but the return trip was hell on tarmac. Every acceleration, every braking was as if my wound was opening up, I could feel even the smallest stone passing under one of the tyres.

After riding on stones for a long time, we arrived home, I arrived pale and holding back the vomit with my hands that wanted to escape from inside my stomach. It was disgusting.

Finally it escaped from inside me and I

was reunited with the smelly, practically digested pieces of fish I had tried to eat days before. That stomacal explosion of liquids and food spilled everywhere and with them, my stapled back suffered a major, thick haemorrhage, full of dark secretions and putrid clots.

The time had come, after returning that majestic feast to the world, to perform the first home treatment.

But not without first collecting the paste that had emerged from within, as if it were the last supper. My little dog, excited, wanted to pay tribute to himself by gulping down that smelly fish paste with the help of his busy tongue.

Maria with extreme care and affection, a quality I could not enjoy during my stay in the hospital, as the nurses performed their mechanised, robotic and unfeeling duties, proceeded to remove the bandana covering my surgical wound and cleaned it. I felt pleasantly comforted and clean, as if I had bathed in crystal clear water. Then I went back to bed. I needed, and was to a few weeks' rest.

CHAPTER XVII
1619-1621

After my well-deserved weeks of rest, one fine morning, and after I had slept that night for what seemed to me endless hours, Maria appeared in the room, with an invitation in hand, reminding me that we had a wedding that weekend.

Looking at the invitation, I remembered that the wedding was to be held about an hour's drive from home in the typical old, lost farmhouse, only connected to civilisation by some narrow, unpaved road.

I had to be very meticulous with all the post-operative medication if I was to have any chance of attending the event.

Victor and Maricarmen were to be united in sacramental marriage. He was a childhood friend like everyone else and Maricarmen was an exceptional person who knew how to make him happy from day one and who, together with Claudia, their daughter, made a beautiful family.

I was especially excited to attend such an important event and to be able to meet up again with my old friends. I was going to be able to enjoy something normal since my life had been caught up in a visceral and agonising slaughter without any foresight.

It saddened me greatly that Alberto, one of my eternal comrades, who had his son Pau a couple of months ago, with Tamara, his wife, could not attend. Pau was too young and the

place was too remote and remote to take any risk if a medical emergency arose, typical of neonates.
But there I was going to meet Carlos and Eva, whom we met on a trip to Malta when we were just young kids on a rampage and if I remember correctly, about twenty years ago.
I would enjoy the always characteristic cultured and refined humour of our friend Héctor, or Tor as he liked to be called, and Miriam, his partner.
I could not forget Martí, the latest addition to that small group of friends, born twenty-five years ago, when several headless teenagers decided to walk as a group, the road to maturity.
So, after a few days, the four of us headed for that inhospitable place.
Maria drove my car one of those all-terrain vehicles that have become so fashionable, and I was grateful, since in that format we would try to make

thefinal stretch of the journey to the location of the junction, in a gentler way.

Finally, after a few endless minutes of mud and stones, a road that never seemed to end where you leave the comfort of the civilitation and it seems that you are driving into the maw of a forest, where the only company was that of the thermometer on the screen of the vehicle,the temperature lowering centigrade every metre as we went deeper into that road.

We arrived at what apparently looked like a rural house, with its thousands of acres, a sort of manor, a place frozen in time where there was neither space nor time to listen to the new oracles, lavishing their words, their truth and their beliefs when asked, in our century, and who respond through loudspeakers that seem sensibly intelligent, but totally mechanical, that too often make the listener doubt between reality and fiction.

There, the only access to information was through large solid wooden gates in the form of arched doors.

When we arrived at the provisional car park to unload our suitcases, we were greeted by a gentleman, one of the old ones, and by old I mean that his face, his clothes worn out by too much work in the fields, and from his right hand hung a sickle.

Without saying a word, he raised his free arm and with his finger, pointed the way to our bedroom and there we went. We did not want to go against someone who welcomed us with a hand occupied by such a weapon, a flayer of men.

We arrived at the main entrance of the farmhouse, an entrance where door groaned as we pushed it, quite hard indeed, in order to enter it.

In front of it we had our room and next to it a service bathroom, small but adequate, an old-fashioned kitchen with a large wood-burning oven, which apparently was used quite often.

We unpacked our luggage quickly, having to hurry because at that moment, I looked at my phone without coverage and its clock alerted me that it was half past four in the afternoon and the ceremony started at six o'clock.

So, with all the haste we could muster, we dressed the children, got ourselves ready and more or less elegantly made our way to the ceremony site, which was about to begin.

On the way to the altar, we came across a kind of stone bench, adorned with two solid wooden posts tied together in the shape of a cross, or rather, in the shape of an 'X', a place where nowadays families usually

picnic and lovers have their first kiss
as husband and wife.
As the curious being that I am, I
approached this place to read a small
plaque that appeared to be
commemorative,
reading as follows:

Here and under this cross, during the
early 17th century, specifically
between 1619 and 1621 a short but
intense witch hunt, ended the lives, by
hanging, of several women, unjustly
accused of witchcraft, some of these
women on trial were....

The moss and the passing of the years
on that old engraved stone plaque did
not allow me to see their names, due
to the deterioration.
Once there and seated in our place,
fourth row from the left, since
according to the priest who was going

to officiate the wedding, the place where one should sit is the one that corresponds to him, no more and no less.

Everything was great, the bride was beautiful, the groom apparently calm and very elegant. They took their vows and we all headed towards the place where a cocktail would be held before dinner.

We walked, I with the help of my cane towards that area, where we were entertained with plenty of food and drink.

While Quim seemed more obsessed with getting, as his only food, some green apples hanging from a tree, Nil, who has always been more formal, enjoyed the cuts of good cured ham. After a few hours and honestly, after having drunk a glass of white wine, I took my medication, a big mistake.

A few minutes later, those present

began to deform their bodies in an impossible way, everything began to spin, and what had been an incredible evening turned into a horrendous nightmare.

The music began to distort, the people who were there, suddenly, with wandering steps and upside down bodies began to chase me, or so it seemed to me, I didn't even have the help of Maria, who together with the children, marched into the room, minutes before, to put them to sleep from such a tired party.

Something was going wrong, and in a mixture of fear and agonised surprise, I too headed for our room.

In a less agile way than I would have liked, I walked the path that separated me from my family, now in the distance and in a static way, seemed to look at me, so as not to lose sight of me. They were not chasing me either. I

understood absolutely nothing.
Once I crossed the imposing cross-shaped masts, which hunted and killed witches centuries before, I arrived at the entrance gates. They creaked and groaned when I opened them, but I didn't even remember it. They put me on alert, their grunts frightening me. Once inside, having crossed that old kitchen, in which now,

The oven, for some strange reason, was burning, fuelled by old wood. I got to my room. I lay down next to them, but the children, Maria... lived oblivious to what had happened, and as always, I thought it was the result of taking my medicine.
In the same way, once covered with the bed sheets, which I used as an improvised shield, I was unable to feel safe, and a few minutes later, trembling, I fell asleep.

After a few hours, at four o'clock in the morning, a scream that seemed to have no source to emit it, made me jump out of my bed, while the others slept soundly and undisturbed. I opened the small porthole of the window we had in our room to see the impossible again. The local man who had given us a warm welcome hours before, and following us with sickle in hand, was shouting out names, meaningless to me, I didn't know them. He was shouting women's names, seeming to chase people who were impossible to see or voices that were unheard by others, except for him, except for me. I simply thought that the old farmer had lost some of his eloquence and that his old head was not working properly. Suddenly a second scream, which I could hear clearly, a screech that sounded grim and mournful, alerted the farmer who ran off following the trail of the screech, disappeared into the trees. That shriek was real, too real, it wasn't me, it wasn't my head or my medication either. I was as crazy as that villager or something was really going on behind that small window. For some strange reason, I made my way to the front door, trying to remember the creaking sound it made when someone tried to open it. This time my way back to the exit had a different detail than before, the kitchen with its glowing wood stove, gave off the smell of meat. Once I had opened the sounding door, in the distance, a farming shadow, with a sickle in his hand, was chasing what seemed to be silhouettes with long coppery hair, I could distinguish them thanks to the powerful full moon that illuminated all those fields that night. Those escaping silhouettes were

laughing at the poor old man who was chasing them, unable to catch up with them while he was cursing them in the name of God.
Evidently I wanted to stay out of that brawl, looking at them from afar with astonishment, suddenly those chased shadows disappeared, suddenly vanished while that man, the flayer of witches, panting from the effort, prayed in the name of the father, of the son... and then collapsed. I shouldn't have seen any of that, I cursed, I went back to my room trying to find a comforting bed next to mine. I opened my door, closed the window shutter, stretched out again with my anaesthetised children, shielded myself again with sheets and more.

Late on, I went back to sleep trembling. The next morning, with a tired face I woke up, Maria and the

children had gone out to breakfast. They were under those old cross masts.
Fantastic, I thought...
There were no nicer places, to have coffee. None of the guests I came across seemed to know anything about what had happened that night, and I didn't want to ask them either, for fear of what they would think of me. I urged my family to finish breakfast quickly so that I could return home, and they agreed with me. When we got into my car and started to drive off, I saw in the rear-view mirror that old man, who hours before had been hunting?
witches?
And who now appeared to be slightly injured. I made the whole trip back without saying a word or ever explaining what had happened to anyone, until now.

CHAPTER XVIII
A Good Father

The cuckoo clock, the next morning, was already warning of the arrival of Father Christmas, that night the good Father Christmas would arrive in his sleigh pulled mainly by Rudolph and would come down the chimneys of all the houses in our small, snowy village. The picture could not have been nicer, like a postcard,
Through the window, the first children in the early morning were already playing with snowballs, whilt others were building snowmen, almost bringing them to life.
The smell of burning wood, produced by the fireplaces at full capacity,

intoxicated the whole atmosphere with its pleasant aroma.

While all this was going on, I sat down in front of the computer, ready to continue with the novel I was writing. My eagerness for it was almost obsessive and Maria reminded me of this, warning me that the children already had their scarves around their necks and were impatient to go out and play in the snow.

So I grabbed my mobile phone to continue writing on it, since it was like an extension of my desktop computer, and I accompanied my children outside, despite the fact that the sky was filled with a radiant sun, almost bluish for the time of year, and it was exaggeratedly cold.

But there I was, with my veteran crutch, tired from what I had experienced, holding the weather for and for the enjoyment of my children,

who cared little about the weather. they didn't care if the thermometer read below zero.
At that moment, static and frozen, it came to my mind for the first time in my life, that I had become a good father, although it was selfish for me to think so. You will have to evaluate that, tomorrow my children. That feeling invaded my body and drew a small smile in the centre of my face and that was a lot, I was not a person who smiled very often and the events lived lately blurred even more any hint of happiness on my face.
I was almost uncapable of remembering what that feeling felt like.

They called it happiness and I had almost forgotten all about it. Suddenly a window in the house opened and powerfully let out the

sweet smell of freshly baked biscuits
in, possibly, Christmas shapes.
Maria, through the window, alerted us
that they were burning but were ready
for us to come in for breakfast.
My deaf children, like most children,
do not listen to their parents'
commands,

They were still oblivious to the outside
world, focussed on playing with the
snow and a small sledge we had.
I headed for the door of the house,
decorated with poinsettias, looking for
a warm place to expel from my body
the cold from the outside that had
already penetrated inside me.
Maria and I took a biscuit each,
standing up because sitting down was
still a pain for my pelvis.
Although the day was perfect, I was
not to forget that I had to be operated
on twice more, that my drugs would

still be there every day waiting to be taken and give birth to their full potential, possibly hallucinogenic or not....

That my poor spine would not support the pins or the vertebral rivets that were attached to it and would have to be opened again, like a zip, but there I was enjoying breakfast with my wife, my head went back to the past, it was like a first date and I should enjoy that company, that biscuit. The rest would come running over my life again, but I didn't deserve to be the main character at that moment, I had no right to be.

My children suddenly entered the house, zombified by the smell of biscuits, ready to leave nothing for the others. I kissed Maria and smiled, this time at my children, while they were already devouring those delicious biscuits that no longer burned so

much, I hugged them, the rest would
come and would be told another time.I
understood that at that moment
I had to enjoy for the last time
that first time.

END

Dear reader:
I hope you enjoyed this little novel, the
first one I've written. Like Bergamo,
we all make mistakes when we are
beginners, in this case of writing,
translation or format, which I hope you
have understood.

But I want you to understand
something and the reason for this
novel.

I don't know how to give up and even
less when I want to, maybe because of
stubbornness or hope.
I don't know, but I'll keep on doing it
and if one day stubbornness abandons
me, begs me to stop and threatens me
that I won't be able to bear one more
wound, my heart will have to explain
to it that I only have one life to try...
That I will have to pursue my dreams,
whatever they may be, unwaveringly,

that I will have to make the stones
stumble if necessary, because in this
life there is nothing left but to be
stubborn until I succeed.
And if victory doesn't come, because
I'm stubborn I'll go for it, even if I'm
broken inside, but in one piece on the
outside, my dear.